HUBERT

THE CATERPILLAR WHO THOUGHT HE WAS A MUSTACHE

BY WENDY STANG AND SUSAN RICHARDS

PICTURES BY ROBERT L. ANDERSON

A Harlin Quist Book

PUBLISHED BY HARLIN QUIST, INC.
DISTRIBUTED BY DIAL / DELACORTE SALES
1 DAG HAMMARSKJOLD PLAZA, NEW YORK 10017
COPYRIGHT © 1967 BY HARLIN QUIST, INC.
ALL RIGHTS RESERVED
LIBRARY OF CONGRESS CARD: AC 67-16284
ISBN PAPERBACK: 0-8252-3475-1
ISBN HARDCOVER: 8-8252-0037-7
FOURTH PRINTING
PRINTED IN THE U.S.A.
DESIGNED BY JOHN BRADFORD

Hubert was a very mixed-up caterpillar.

He
thought
he
was
a
mustache.
Of course,
it's plain
to
see
why.

When Hubert
was at a party,
he was always
left alone.
Because when
he was introduced as
Hubert The Caterpillar,
he would reply proudly,
"I'm not a caterpillar.
I'm a mustache."

"Everyone knows,"
thought everyone else,
"that a caterpillar
is a caterpillar and
only a caterpillar."

Hubert was
very unhappy.

"I'M A MUSTACHE."

*One day
Hubert
was
walking
along
dreaming
of a face
he might
someday
wear.*

Suddenly Hubert felt himself being lifted into the air! He shut his eyes tight!

Hubert was frightened.
Then he opened his eyes
and found himself
in a very dark box.

He explored the box
and discovered it
was unlatched.
He could escape!
Now was his chance
to find a face!

Walking across a desk,
Hubert glanced up and
saw an immense face
staring at him.
He slowly crawled up
and settled himself
on the face's upper lip.
Hubert was excited!

Then Hubert realized
it was only a photograph!
He was very unhappy.

Then he saw another face.
Encouraged, he squirmed
towards it. He crawled up
the arm and reached the
face and placed himself
where a mustache
ought to be.

But—oh, my!—
Hubert had made
another mistake.
It was only a doll.

But Hubert
would not give up.

He wandered about
a bit until he came
upon a very large nose.
Hubert decided
to give it a try.

Suddenly something awful happened! The nose sneezed!

Hubert found himself
across the room.
He was tired and
unhappy. So he
crawled back into
the box, feeling
sleepy and sad.

When he awoke
something strange
had happened!
He was not
the same Hubert!

*He
was
a butterfly!*

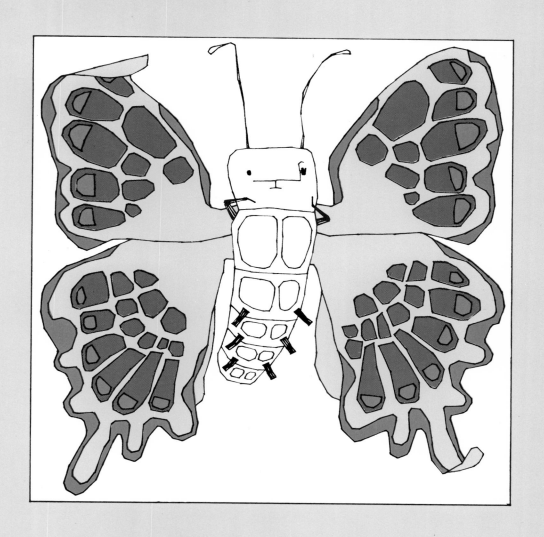

When
he
looked
at
his
wings,
Hubert
no longer
thought
he was a
mustache.

Now Hubert thinks he's an eagle!

And he is very happy.